STRIKER'S SISTER

BY JAKE MADDOX

text by Emma Carlson Berne
illustrated by Katie Wood

STONE ARCH BOOKS
a capstone imprint

Jake Maddox Girl Sports Stories are published by Stone Arch Books
a Capstone imprint
1710 Roe Crest Drive
North Mankato, Minnesota 56003
www.mycapstone.com

Library of Congress Cataloging-in-Publication Data is available
on the Library of Congress website.

ISBN: 978-1-4965-6355-2 (library binding)
ISBN: 978-1-4965-6357-6 (paperback)
ISBN: 978-1-4965-6359-0 (ebook PDF)

Summary: Lily's older sister, Jana, has recently left home for basic
training, and Lily really misses her soccer idol. And when Lily's parents
and coach start pushing her to fill Jana's cleats, the pressure to be like
the all-star striker is too much. Can Lily find the strength to be herself?

Designers: Ted Williams and Laura Manthe
Production Specialist: Tori Abraham
Design Elements: Shutterstock

Printed and bound in Canada.
PA020

TABLE OF CONTENTS

CHAPTER ONE

MISSING JANA

"Lily, heads-up!" Mari yelled.

Cowboys goalie Lily Davis watched as the Bobcat striker dribbled down the field. The girl's eyes were fixed and determined.

Lily stood between the goalposts and tried to focus. Behind her, the white net rippled in the warm fall breeze. The green turf stretched before her.

Lily's teammate Susannah ran forward. She shifted left and right. Then she darted in like a dragonfly and stole the ball away.

Another Bobcat rushed toward Susannah. She took the ball back and dodged around the Cowboys' defenders.

The Bobcats were getting close to the goal box again. Lily narrowed her eyes.

Lily had always felt best between the metal bars of the goal. After all, she had been playing goalie since she was six. The goal box felt like a second home.

But everything was different now.

The Bobcat striker smacked the ball at the net. Lily jumped sideways.

THUMP!

The ball smacked into her hands, as it had done a hundred times before. This time, though, the thrill was missing. Lily booted the ball back into play. But all the passion and game had drained out of her.

It was all because her big sister, Jana, was gone. Lily knew that was the problem. Her sister wasn't practicing on the next field. She wasn't sitting in the bleachers. This was Lily's first game of the new season and the first time ever Jana wasn't there.

At the thought of her sister, Lily's throat tightened. She tried to watch the game in front of her. But her teammates became blurry as her eyes filled with tears.

Jana had left for Army boot camp three days ago. She was two states away, doing push-ups. Or whatever people did in boot camp. She had called only once.

Lily remembered the conversation. "Mom? It's Jana," she'd said. "I've arrived. I'll call within seventy-two hours with my address. Make sure you have a pen when I call. I have to go. Love you."

That was it. Now they were waiting for the second call.

Lily missed her sister so much. Everyone missed Jana—Mom and Dad, her friends, even the soccer coach. Her absence was like a gaping hole everywhere Lily turned.

Lily quickly wiped away her tears. "Goalie!" someone shouted, and the field snapped back into focus.

The ball was flying toward her. Lily jumped left with her hands outstretched. But the ball sailed past them. It snagged in the goal net.

"Yes!" the Bobcat striker yelled. The Bobcats ran together for a group hug.

Lily picked herself up off the ground. The Cowboys slowly walked back to their positions. No one looked at her.

They didn't have to. Lily knew she had messed up. She hadn't been paying attention. She had let an easy shot through.

Jana never would've lost focus like that, Lily thought. *Even though she was a striker, she always kept her head in the game.*

Shame rose up inside of Lily. The game had only just started. But Lily knew that for her, it was already over.

CHAPTER TWO

FILLING A SISTER'S CLEATS

Lily struggled to finish the match. She blocked a few more shots, but one snuck in during the final minutes. When the whistle blew, the score was 1–2. The Bobcats won.

Lily tried to hold back the tears. She hadn't cried over a missed save in years. She kept her face down as the Cowboys lined up for the handshakes. Her best friend, Charlotte, got behind her.

"Lils, are you OK?" Charlotte asked as they slapped the hands of the Bobcats.

"Yeah, I'm—" Lily stopped. She couldn't talk without crying.

As soon as Lily had gotten through the handshake line, she ran off the field. She didn't even wait for Charlotte.

She grabbed her soccer bag from the locker room and left before her teammates came in. She didn't want to talk to anyone. They'd just see her red eyes and feel sorry for her.

Lily hurried out to the parking lot. She leaned her head against the warm metal of Mom's car. Tears ran down her cheeks. She felt like an overflowing cup.

Then she heard her mom's voice. "Oh, Lily," Mom said. "It's all right."

Lily turned and saw her parents. She hugged them both tightly.

"It just feels so weird to play without Jana," Lily said with a sniff. "I miss her so much."

Mom's eyes glittered with tears. "I know," she said. "We miss her too."

The hard knot inside Lily relaxed a little. Her parents understood. They felt the same way. For a moment, they all stood together in a big hug.

"But it'll be OK," Dad said. "We still have you here. You'll be our soccer all-star now. You'll be just like Jana."

"What?" Lily asked, stepping back. She wasn't sure she'd heard him correctly.

"That's right," Mom added. She tucked a strand of hair back into Lily's braids. "You'll fill your sister's shoes, Lils. That'll help us all."

Lily blinked hard. She'd never felt so odd. *I miss Jana*, she thought, *but I don't want to be her.* She had to get away. She had to think.

Mom opened the car door. "Come on, let's get a bite before we go home."

"N-no thanks," Lily stammered. "I think I'll walk."

"Oh!" Mom said. "Are you sure?"

"Yep, I just need some air," Lily called over her shoulder. She was already hurrying away. "See you at home!"

She wondered if they could hear the falseness in her voice the way she could. Or if they were even hearing her at all.

CHAPTER THREE

SOCCER LEGACY

A few minutes later, Lily shoved open the big blue school doors. She had been planning on going straight home. But something seemed to pull her back toward the school.

Glass cases as tall as her lined the hallway near the locker rooms. Overhead, the ceiling was draped in the blue and white Cowboys flags.

The hall was empty. Lily's teammates had already changed and gone home.

The only sound was Lily's footsteps on the polished cement floor.

Lily took a deep breath and blew it out through her lips. It was a technique Jana had taught Lily to slow her breathing. It always helped Lily calm down.

Lily walked slowly past the cases. There were debate team trophies, plaques for swimming, and honor certificates in English. She stopped in front of the third display case.

Soccer plaques were lined up on the top row, like soldiers. Lily read the writing on each one.

Jana Davis, Most Valuable Player—Offense.

Jana Davis, All-American Girls Varsity Soccer.

That last one had been right before Jana left for boot camp.

There were also team awards. They didn't have Jana's name on them. But she had led those teams. Those were her awards too.

"Lils!" a voice called.

Lily turned. Charlotte was trotting down the hall, carrying her soccer bag.

"I waited and waited for you!" Charlotte said. "Where did you go?"

Lily didn't reply. She just groaned as she slid down onto the floor. She tilted her head back against the glass case.

Charlotte dropped down beside her friend. "What's wrong?" she asked.

"Oh, Char!" Lily cried. "I don't know what's happening! I miss Jana so much that I can't play. That's one thing. But now it seems like Mom and Dad want me to *be* Jana. They told me I have to fill her shoes."

Charlotte listened silently. Her normally cheerful face was serious.

"I don't want to fill Jana's shoes. I'm not her!" Lily continued. "I couldn't be her even if I wanted to." She swept a hand up toward the glittering trophy case.

"Of course you shouldn't have to be like Jana," Charlotte said. "You're great like you are. When have we ever had a better goalie?"

"Not today," Lily mumbled. Then she added, "But Mom and Dad miss her so much. Maybe I should just do what they want. Maybe I'll try to be like Jana."

"But you're not Jana. You're *you*," Charlotte said firmly. "That's why you're my best friend. And don't you forget it either."

Lily hugged Charlotte. "Thanks," she said. "You always know what to say. Want to walk home with me?"

Her friend nodded and smiled, and Lily smiled back. At least Charlotte liked her for who she was. If only she could be so sure that everyone else felt the same way.

CHAPTER FOUR

CHANGE UP

"Ugh!" Lily yelled as she dove forward at the next day's practice.

She caught the ball and then jumped to her feet. She rolled it back to her team.

The Cowboys were running a kicking drill. Lily was easily blocking most of the shots. She was feeling better today.

I just need to keep my mind on soccer, she told herself. *Don't worry about Jana, or what Mom and Dad said. Everything will be fine. Just focus on the field.*

Coach Rose blew her whistle. "Let's move on to the scrimmage! Lily, you'll be striker now. Charlotte, take over goal for Lily. Susannah will be in the opposite goal."

The coach divided the rest of the girls into two teams. When she was done, everyone ran to their spots.

Lily got into the striker position. It felt weird to be out on the field. She almost never left the goal. But Coach wanted to train Charlotte as a backup goalkeeper.

The scrimmage started. Soon Nora, who was on Lily's team, had the ball. She dodged Abbie and passed to Mari.

Mari moved to pick up the pass, but Becca immediately swooped in. Becca got her cleat on the ball. She turned it around and dribbled up the field.

Lily ran after her. Becca was fast, but Lily was faster.

Lily clenched her fists and pumped her arms and legs. She quickly caught up with the other girl. She stuck her foot out and scooped the ball away from Becca.

Behind her, Lily could hear Nora and Mari cheer. She rushed toward the goal.

Abbie darted in front of her and tried to stop the attack. But Lily faked to the left, and then easily spun around her opponent. Lily kept running forward.

The goal was wide open. No defenders were in Lily's way. Charlotte got ready with her hands out.

But Lily knew just how to get the ball around the goalie. She drew her leg back and booted the ball hard.

Charlotte jumped, but she couldn't reach high enough. The ball spun past her and right into the upper right corner of the net.

"Whoo!" Mari cheered from the field. "Wow, that was nice!"

"Yeah," Charlotte added as she came out of the goal. "Good power at the end, Lils."

"Thanks," Lily panted.

As Lily looked toward the sideline, she caught Coach Rose's gaze. Coach stared at Lily for a long minute. Then she marked something on her clipboard.

The Cowboys continued their scrimmage. Both teams got in a few shots. Lily even picked up another goal in the last minute. Soon Coach Rose blew her whistle.

"Team, gather round!" she yelled.

The girls huddled together.

"As you know, the first game of the Crosstown Fall Tournament is Saturday," Coach Rose said. "We'll be playing the Forest Hills Thunder. They're fast, but they tend to be careless. Here are the positions."

She began reading names off her clipboard. "Becca, forward. Lily, striker. Charlotte, goalie."

The coach was still talking, but Lily didn't hear anything else. *Did she say I was striker?* she thought.

Lily raised her hand. "Um, Coach?"

"Yes, Davis?" she said.

"I'm sorry, but did you mean Charlotte is striker and I'm goalie?" Lily asked.

Coach Rose shook her head. "No. I want to switch things up for the tournament. It'll give both of you some good practice."

Lily stared at Charlotte over on the other side of the huddle. Charlotte's wide eyes stared back.

Striker was Jana's position. She'd always been striker, and Lily had always been goalie.

It seemed like Lily was going to be like Jana, whether she wanted to or not.

CHAPTER FIVE

JANA'S JERSEY

"How was practice, Lils?" Mom asked that night at dinner.

Lily looked up from her enchiladas and green beans. She had been pushing the food around on her plate. She wasn't hungry. Not after the shock from practice.

"It was . . . weird," she replied.

But weird didn't even begin to describe it. She couldn't stop thinking about her new position.

"What do you mean? Weird how?" asked her dad.

"Coach wants to switch up positions for the Crosstown Fall Tournament," Lily explained. "She's putting Charlotte as goalie and moving me to striker."

Her parents' faces lit up. "Jana's position!" Mom said. "That's wonderful!"

"I was kind of bummed, actually," Lily mumbled. "I love goalie."

"Striker is an honor. That's what Jana always thought," Dad said. He grinned. "Channeling your big sister, huh?"

"B-but . . . ," Lily stammered helplessly.

Her parents weren't even looking at her. They were looking at each other.

"Phil, do you think it's time?" Mom said.

"Just what I was thinking! I'll get it," Dad said, springing up from his chair.

They heard his feet on the stairs a moment later.

Soon Dad was rushing back into the room. He had something in his hands. With a big smile, he held it up.

Lily stared. Her stomach suddenly felt as if it were filled with concrete instead of food. It was Jana's old jersey. The dark number 4 stood out against the light blue.

Dad held out the jersey. Like a robot, Lily automatically took it.

"Jana asked us to give it to you after she left," Mom explained. "She thought you might like to keep it. But now that you're playing Jana's old position . . . you could wear it in games! Try it on!"

Lily slipped the mesh fabric over her head. The scent of lavender wafted up. It was Jana's body wash. She never used any other kind.

"Just a little big," Dad said. "Isn't it nice we can still feel close to your sister, even when she's far away?"

"Yeah," Lily choked out. She felt like she'd scream if she stayed there for one more second. "I should go upstairs. I have lots of homework to do."

She managed to hold back the tears until she was in her room.

* * *

In the locker room the next day, Lily's stomach flipped as she unzipped her soccer bag. Jana's jersey was right on top.

Lily wanted to hide it away in her room, but Mom and Dad had been so excited to give it to her. She couldn't bring herself to leave it at home.

She shook it out and could still smell the lavender scent. Luckily she wouldn't have to wear it for today's practice.

"Oh my gosh, is that Jana's jersey?" someone asked as Lily was about to hang it in her locker.

Lily looked over her shoulder. Mari was coming over.

"Oh, yeah but—" Lily started to say.

"That's awesome!" Mari said. She admired the jersey with a big grin.

"Hey!" Coach Rose said as she came out of her office. "All right, number four! Are you going to wear it on Saturday's game?"

"Um, maybe I shouldn't?" Lily asked. "It's a different number, and I don't want to cause any problems."

Coach waved a hand. "Oh no, go ahead! It'd be great to honor your sister like that. I'll just change your number on the paperwork. It's like having our old girl back!"

But what about this *girl?* Lily thought as she put the jersey away. *I miss Jana too, but isn't anyone glad I'm here?*

CHAPTER SIX

DISAPPEARING

In the middle of practice, Coach Rose blew her whistle. "Shooting drills. Let's hustle!"

Charlotte threw Lily an apologetic look as she ran to the goal. Lily lined up with the rest of the team. It felt wrong not to be in the goalie box.

Abbie was first to take a shot. She ran forward and booted the ball. Charlotte leapt sideways. But she missed it.

Charlotte should've kicked it out! Lily couldn't help thinking. She could almost *feel* the right movement in her body.

Mari dribbled up next. Charlotte managed to block the shot, but just barely. Lily could see the sweat shining on her friend's face.

Soon Lily was at the head of the line. She ran up and aimed a kick.

Before her foot even hit the ball, Lily could tell it wasn't going to be a good shot. She thumped it off-center. The ball spun weakly toward the goal.

Coach tweeted her whistle. "Try it again, Lily!" she called.

Lily felt her face burn. She didn't look at her teammates as she dribbled the ball back into position.

Come on! she told herself. She didn't need to add public embarrassment to her list of current problems.

She shoved all the thoughts out of her head and ran forward. Legs pumping, she hit the ball hard. The laces of her cleat hit it with a satisfying *thwack*.

The ball shot toward the corner of the goal. Charlotte leapt and reached—and missed.

"Good job, Jana!" Coach Rose yelled.

Lily froze. *What did she just say?*

"Sorry, I mean Lily, of course," the coach corrected. She smiled at her. "I knew you'd be great at striker. It's in your blood!"

Coach Rose blew her whistle again. "All right, let's move on to the scrimmage!"

The practice seemed to drag on forever. During the scrimmage, Lily kept glancing at the space between the goalposts. That used to be her territory.

It was a lot of responsibility to play goalkeeper, but Lily had always loved stepping up for her team. Nothing was better than when she jumped for the ball. She'd soar through the air. Then she'd feel the thump in her gloves and hear the cheers from the stands.

Lily felt the pressure building inside her as she ran down the field. Voices seemed to echo inside her head. *You'll be just like Jana!* her dad's voice said. *Good job, Jana!* added Coach Rose.

Becca shot the ball to her. Lily trapped it, then dribbled toward the goal.

It was as if Jana was a ghost. She was in the jersey and in everyone's mind, but she wasn't there. Now Lily was beginning to feel like *she* wasn't really there either. She was disappearing.

Lily smacked the ball. It soared past Charlotte's hands and into the net. Her teammates cheered, but Lily didn't feel happy. Instead her stomach twisted.

I love soccer, and I love this team! Lily thought. *But how can I keep playing like this?*

CHAPTER SEVEN

A MESSAGE

"Hello!" Mom called from the kitchen as Lily opened the door after practice.

"Hi," Lily muttered.

She immediately turned toward the stairs. The last thing she wanted was a cheerful conversation with Mom about practice. She didn't want to hear how excited everyone was for Saturday's game.

The mail slot clicked open. Several letters and catalogs thumped onto the doormat.

"Is that the mail?" Mom called again. "Can you pick it up, honey?"

Sighing, Lily scooped up the pile. There was a gardening catalog for Dad and two credit card ad. Then Lily stopped.

It was a letter from Jana. And it was addressed to Lily.

Lily dumped the rest of the mail on the hall table. Then she rushed up the stairs and into her room. She sank onto her bed.

Slowly, she tore open the envelope.

Hi, Lily!

Sorry I haven't written before now. They keep us really busy in basic training, but I'm holding up OK. They just started allowing us letters once a week. You get the first one! Don't worry, I'll write Mom and Dad next time.

I've been thinking about you and the team constantly. How are the Cowboys shaping up this year? It's so weird not to be there. I can't believe this is the first year I haven't played soccer since I was five!

Have Mom and Dad given you my old jersey? I thought you might like to hang on to it. But I know you'll be on the field rocking it out in your own goalie jersey! I'm bummed I can't watch your awesome saves. I still remember when you first put on the goalkeeper gloves. You were sort of scared. Remember how you told me it was like the whole opposing team was running at you at the same time?

But you stuck with it and didn't give up and practiced like crazy. Now you own that goal! I want you to remember that coming up to the Crosstown Tournament.

I'm so proud of you, Lily. You kill it on Saturday, OK?

Love, love, love,

Jana

Lily stared at the letter for a long time. A tear dripped off the end of her nose and hit the paper. She'd give anything to hug her sister right now.

Jana wasn't there, but Lily had her letter. And her sister believed in her.

Jana doesn't want me to be another Jana, Lily thought. She held the letter tightly in her hands. *She wants me to be my own self— Lily. And I want that too.*

She knew what she had to do.

CHAPTER EIGHT

SPEAKING UP

Lily stood in front of Mom and Dad, who sat together on the couch. They both frowned with concern. Mom was still wiping her hands on a dishcloth. Dad had only just gotten home from work.

"What did you want to talk to us about, Lils?" Mom asked. "Is something wrong?"

Lily squeezed Jana's letter. She had folded it up into a small square, like some kind of good luck charm.

"No," Lily replied. "I mean, yes. I mean, soon there won't be."

Her parents looked even more confused.

Lily took a deep breath. She looked her parents in the eye. It was hard.

"I've been feeling weird about soccer lately," she started. "I love playing, but things are different now. Jana's gone. And it seems like everyone—you guys, Coach, the team—wants me to take her place."

Mom started to speak, but Lily shook her head. "Mom, wait. I'm going to cry unless I just say this, OK? I mean, I'm playing striker, and you guys wanted me to wear Jana's jersey. Coach even called me Jana the other day. And the thing is . . ."

Lily paused. "I don't want to be Jana. I want to be myself. I want to be a goalie, not a striker. I don't want to wear Jana's jersey. I want to wear my own."

Her parents were silent. "Why didn't you tell us this sooner?" Mom finally asked.

Lily smiled a little. "I didn't have the courage. Until I got this letter."

She gave it to her parents and waited while they read.

Mom sighed. "Lils, we are so sorry. Dad and I never meant for you to think we want you to be Jana. Of course, we want you to be *you*. That's the Lily we love."

"We didn't realize what we were doing," Dad added. "We've been thinking about Jana a lot. I guess it all spilled over."

"I know you both love me the way I am," Lily said. She swallowed. "It just . . . hasn't felt that way lately."

Mom stood and pulled Lily into a hug. Lily rested her head on Mom's shoulder.

"Well, what are you going to do now?" Mom asked.

Lily straightened up. She felt stronger already. "I have a plan," she said. "First, I have to text Charlotte."

* * *

Charlotte came right over after Lily texted. Lily was already waiting for her outside on the lawn.

"Hey, Lily. What's up?" Charlotte asked.

"Listen, Char. I've been feeling awful as striker," Lily told her. "Would you be OK with switching positions? Then we can ask Coach about it."

"Of course! I could see how bad you felt, Lils," Charlotte said. "Plus I hate goalie! Do you think Coach will let us switch?"

"It's worth a try," Lily said.

They went inside. Lily took out her phone and brought up Coach Rose's number. Then she hit call.

Lily put the phone on speaker. When the coach answered, she listened carefully while the two girls explained everything. Then Lily made her request.

"Thanks for telling me your concerns. I'll think about this carefully," Coach said. "I'll post the positions in the locker room tomorrow morning."

CHAPTER NINE

BETWEEN THE GOALPOSTS

Early the next morning, Lily was already pulling on her shin guards. She couldn't wait for the game today.

As she walked to school, she reminded herself not to get too excited. Maybe Coach Rose would keep her as striker. But she just had a feeling that her plan had worked.

The locker room was quiet when she came in. She had the place to herself.

The roster was on the wall, right where Coach promised. Lily's heart beat fast as she scanned the list.

The words jumped out at her. *Charlotte Edwards, striker. Lily Davis, goalie.*

Lily smiled and pumped her fist. But she didn't have any more time for celebration. The locker room door banged open, and the team began pouring in. They were shouting and laughing. Everyone was excited for the first day of the tournament.

Lily found Charlotte in the crowd and pulled her into a hug. "Coach listened to us!" she exclaimed.

"That's awesome! I knew she would," Charlotte said. "Are you ready to play?"

Lily nodded. "For the first time this season, I really feel like I am."

She took her sister's letter from her bag and folded it into a tiny square. She tucked it into her right shin guard.

Then she pulled out her own goalie jersey and slid it over her head.

* * *

Fweet!

The ref's whistle blew. The Cowboys had the starting kick-off, so Becca passed the ball to Nora. The team quickly dribbled down the field.

Lily carefully watched the action from the goal box. She felt excited and focused. She was finally home.

Late in the first half, Charlotte took the ball close to the Thunder's goal. But a Thunder was on her instantly. She dodged right, then tapped the ball across to Nora.

Nora tried to pass back to Becca, but it rolled out of bounds. It was Thunder's ball.

Each Cowboy got ready and guarded her player. The Thunder midfielder threw the ball.

A Thunder player ran forward to get it, but Mari swooped in. She nabbed the ball and dribbled away. In the stands, the crowd of Cowboys parents cheered.

Mari passed the ball. Charlotte took it and booted it at the Thunder's goal.

Goal! The team ran together. They hugged and high-fived. The score was 1–0.

From the goal box, Lily clapped and cheered. "Nice job, Charlotte!" she shouted.

The Cowboys were playing hard, but so were the Thunder players. The teams continued to move the ball back and forth across the field, but no one scored.

At the start of the second half, Lily had to block two tough shots. Each time the ball thumped into her gloves, she felt that familiar thrill. It was good to be back.

During the second half, a Thunder midfielder got a foot on the ball. She brought it down the field. Lily got ready.

The Thunder whacked the ball toward the goal. Lily flung herself down to the left, but the ball rolled under her and into the net.

It was a Thunder goal. The score was now tied, 1–1.

As Lily got to her feet, though, she didn't feel disappointed. She felt determined.

Lily eyed the clock as the Cowboys took the kick-off and dribbled the ball down the field. Only a few minutes remained in the second half.

Her teammates tried to attack, but the referee blew her whistle. The game was over, and it was still tied.

The team jogged toward the sidelines. Everyone gathered around Coach Rose.

"All right," she said. "You know what's going to happen now. It's a sudden-death tournament, so there can't be a tie. We're going into a penalty shootout."

A sigh went through the team. During a shootout, five players from each team took turns taking a shot directly at the goal. Only the goalie would be there to protect the net. The team with the most goals out of five would win.

Everyone looked at Lily. She swallowed.

"I can do it, guys," she said. Now was her chance to show what she could do.

CHAPTER TEN

LILY DAVIS, GOALIE

Lily positioned herself on the goal line. Both teams stood in the center of the field. A Thunder player walked up for the first kick.

Lily's heart pounded in her ears. The sound was so loud she could barely hear the ref's whistle. The player booted the ball.

Right! Lily's mind screamed as she launched her body to the side.

The ball thumped into her hands.

Blocked! Lily let out a shaky breath as she jogged out of the goal.

The Thunder goalie ran in. Charlotte took the Cowboys' first kick. It burst into the goal. Score!

The team cheered, but then they fell silent. It was Lily's turn in the goal. Blocked. Nora took the next shot for the Cowboys. Blocked. Lily's turn. The ball went in.

Kick by kick, each team took their turn. Sweat dripped down Lily's forehead.

Soon it was 3–2, with the Cowboys in the lead. Four players on each team had taken a shot. If Lily could block this next one, the Thunder wouldn't be able to outscore them. The Cowboys would win.

Lily stood in front of the net. She breathed in deep and blew it out, the way Jana had taught her. She thought of the countless hours she'd put into practice. All her hard work. She was ready.

The Thunder walked forward. The sound on the field seemed to grow muffled. Lily heard a loud hum in her ears. She couldn't see anything except the ball and the Thunder player in red.

Lily crouched down. She held her gloved hands out wide. She bounced on her toes, preparing to make a move.

The Thunder backed away from the ball. Then she ran forward like a freight train.

Bam! The ball shot through the air.

Low! Lily's mind screamed.

She flung herself forward. The ball thumped into her hands as her face scraped the ground.

The field and sidelines erupted in cheers. The Cowboys swarmed around Lily, helping her to her feet.

"You did it!" Mari shrieked. "We're going on to the next round in the tournament!"

"Nice work, goalie!" Charlotte yelled.

Lily realized she was shaking. She raised a trembling hand and wiped the dirt off the side of her face. Charlotte's words echoed in her mind.

Nice work, goalie. She'd saved the game. And she did it as goalie.

Lily could feel Jana's letter tucked under her shin guard. Even though Jana was far away, she was still here—and Lily just knew she was smiling.

Author Bio

Emma Carlson Berne has written over eighty books for children and young adults, including novels, histories, biographies, and short stories. She lives in Cincinnati, Ohio, with her husband and three little boys. When she isn't writing, Emma loves to horseback ride and walk in the woods.

Illustrator Bio

Katie Wood fell in love with drawing when she was very small. Since graduating from Loughborough University School of Art and Design in 2004, she has been living her dream working as a freelance illustrator. From her studio in Leicester, England, she creates bright and lively illustrations for books and magazines all over the world.

Glossary

boot camp (BOOT KAMP)—the training period for people who join the military

cleat (KLEET)—a shoe with spikes on the bottom to help players stop and turn quickly

defender (di-FEND-uhr)—a player whose job is to stop the other team from scoring

drill (DRIL)—a repetitive exercise that helps you learn a specific skill

goalkeeper (GOHL-keep-uhr)—a player who guards the net and tries to stop the other team's shots from going in; also called goalie

position (puh-ZISH-uhn)—a player's role and responsibilities on a team

roster (ROSS-tur)—a list of players on a team

scrimmage (SKRIM-ij)—a practice game

striker (STRAHY-ker)—a player who tries to score goals; also called a forward

Discussion Questions

1. In your own words, describe why Lily was feeling sad throughout the story. What in the text makes you think that? How did Lily solve her problem?

2. Jana mentions in her letter that when Lily first played goalie, Lily felt scared. Discuss a time you tried something new, and how it felt.

3. What are the best parts of having brothers and sisters? What are some of the challenges? If you're an only child, what's fun and challenging about that? Talk about it!

Writing Prompts

1. Pretend you're Lily, and write a letter back to Jana. Tell her how the tournament went, and be sure to let Jana know how her letter helped you.

2. Everyone has their own strengths and interests. Make a list of at least five things that make you unique.

3. Sports should be fun whether your team wins or loses. Write a new ending in which the Cowboys don't win. How might this story still have a happy ending? Use dialogue and descriptive words to make your story come to life.

Soccer Fun Facts

- Soccer has been played as far back as the 1400s, when villages would play ball games together. Sometimes teams had hundreds of players, and the goals might be miles apart! The ball was often a pig's bladder filled with dried peas.

- Soccer is known as *football* in most countries. The United States, Canada, Australia, New Zealand, and South Africa are among the few that call it *soccer*.

- The word *soccer* comes from *association football*, coined by the British in the mid-19th century. Eventually the phrase was shortened to *soc* from the s-o-c in *association*. Later in the 19th century, *soc* turned into *soccer*.

- Soccer is the world's most popular sport. More than 240 million people play some form of soccer.

- A women's World Cup soccer tournament was not held until 1991. That's 61 years after the first men's World Cup.

- In 1999, the U.S. Women's National Team beat China in the final World Cup match. One billion people worldwide watched it on TV, setting a record for the most people viewing a women's sporting event.

- Soccer did not become an Olympic sport for women until 1996. Men have played soccer in the Olympics since 1900.

- Professional soccer players run an average of seven miles during a game.

GIRLS
with
GAME

READ MORE
JAKE MADDOX
STORIES!